THIS BOOK BELONGS TO

_____

PEANUTS®
It's the Great Pumpkin,
CHARLIE BROWN

By Charles M. Schulz
Adapted by Kara McMahon
Illustrated by Scott Jeralds

Simon Spotlight
New York   London   Toronto   Sydney   New Delhi

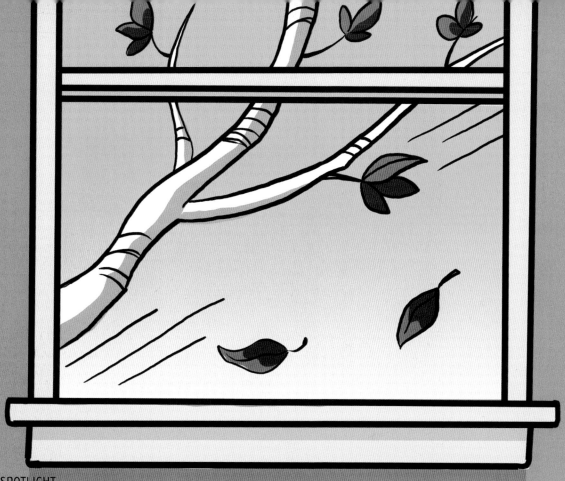

SIMON SPOTLIGHT

An imprint of Simon & Schuster Children's Publishing Division
1230 Avenue of the Americas, New York, New York 10020
First Simon Spotlight edition July 2015

SIMON SPOTLIGHT and colophon are registered trademarks of Simon & Schuster, Inc. For information about special discounts for bulk purchases, please contact Simon & Schuster Special Sales at 1-866-506-1949 or business@simonandschuster.com. Manufactured in China 0520 LEO
10 9   ISBN 978-1-4814-3585-7   ISBN 978-1-4814-3586-4 (eBook)

Every fall, the leaves on the trees turn brown and fall off the branches. Pumpkins grow big and plump in their patches. The air grows cooler, and people start to think about their Halloween costumes. And every fall, Linus writes a very important letter.

Dear Great Pumpkin, Linus writes, *I'm looking forward to your arrival on Halloween night. I hope you will bring me lots of presents.*

"Who are you writing to?" asks Charlie Brown.

"The Great Pumpkin!" Linus replies. "On Halloween night, the Great Pumpkin rises out of his pumpkin patch and flies through the air with his bag of toys for all the children."

Linus's sister, Lucy, isn't happy that Linus is writing to the Great Pumpkin. "You'll make me the laughing stock of the neighborhood!" she complains.

But Charlie Brown's sister, Sally, doesn't think Linus is crazy. She thinks Linus is wonderful. He is her sweet babboo!

"Wouldn't you like to sit with me in the pumpkin patch on Halloween night and wait for the Great Pumpkin?" Linus asks.

Sally is thrilled. "I'd love to," she tells Linus.

Later that day, Charlie Brown has a surprise waiting for him in the mailbox.
"I got an invitation to a Halloween party!" he exclaims.

Lucy thinks the invitation must be a mistake. "There were two lists," she tells
Charlie Brown. "One to invite, and one not to invite."

Charlie Brown knows which list he was probably on. But he decides to go to
the party anyway!

On Halloween night, everyone is planning to go to the party . . . except Linus. "My blockhead brother will be out in the pumpkin patch making his yearly fool of himself," Lucy grumbles. She can't understand why Linus would choose to miss out on all the fun that Halloween has to offer by sitting around in a pumpkin patch.

Everyone puts on their costumes. Lucy is dressed as a witch. Charlie Brown is dressed as a ghost, but no one can tell what he is supposed to be because he had some trouble with the scissors. Sally is also dressed as a ghost, and so is Schroeder. They figured out how to use the scissors just fine. Pigpen is dressed as a ghost too. Everyone can tell which ghost he is because a cloud of dust surrounds him.

Snoopy walks by, also dressed in a costume.
"Who in the world is that?" asks Lucy.
"He's a World War One Flying Ace," Charlie Brown explains.
"Now I've seen everything," Lucy says.

Lucy declares that everyone will go trick-or-treating first and then go to the Halloween party. As they pass by the pumpkin patch, Linus sees them and gets excited, thinking they have come to wait with him. "Have you come to sing pumpkin carols with me?" he asks.

"You blockhead!" Lucy yells at her brother. "You're going to miss all the fun, just like last year!"

"Don't talk like that!" Linus cries. "The Great Pumpkin will come because I am in the most sincere pumpkin patch!"

"Oh good grief!" Lucy exclaims. She marches off with her friends. It looks like no one wants to join Linus in the pumpkin patch to wait for the Great Pumpkin.

Except, what about Sally?

Sally is torn. She doesn't want to miss out on all the fun of trick-or-treating and a party, but Linus is her sweet babboo! What should she do?

Sally runs back to the pumpkin patch.

"I'm glad you came back," Linus tells her. "You'll see the Great Pumpkin with your own eyes!"

Linus is positive the Great Pumpkin will pick this patch. Why wouldn't he? The Great Pumpkin chooses the most sincere patch to visit every year, and how could a pumpkin patch be more sincere than this one?

Sally hopes Linus is right.

Meanwhile, the rest of the kids go trick-or-treating. "Tricks or treats, money or eats!" they yell at the first door.

Everyone compares what they got.

"I got five pieces of candy!" brags Lucy.

"I got a chocolate bar!" exclaims Patty.

"I got a quarter," says Violet happily.

"I got a rock," says Charlie Brown sadly.

And that happens at every door. All the other kids get wonderful treats like candy, gum, and popcorn balls . . . and Charlie Brown gets rocks.

Lucy decides they have done enough trick-or-treating and it's time to go to the party. After all, everyone has a bag filled to the brim with treats. Everyone except Charlie Brown. He has a bag full of rocks.

On their way to the party, they pass by the pumpkin patch again. The kids laugh at Linus and Sally for waiting there instead of coming to the party.

"The Great Pumpkin will be here!" Sally yells, defending Linus.

After the kids walk by, Sally turns to Linus. "All right, where is he?" she asks.

"He'll be here!" Linus assures her.

"I hope so," Sally replies. "Think of all the fun we're missing."

And the Halloween party is a lot of fun . . . for everyone except Charlie Brown. At first Charlie Brown thinks his night is looking up when the other kids ask him to be the model for the jack-o'-lantern. That sounds like a great honor! But then he realizes that being the model means having Violet draw a big pumpkin face on the back of his head.

Meanwhile, in the pumpkin patch, Sally is growing tired of waiting for the Great Pumpkin. "If anyone had told me I'd be waiting in a pumpkin patch on Halloween night, I'd have said they were crazy," she complains.

Just then she and Linus hear a rumbling noise. They see a shadow emerging from the pumpkin patch. "It's the Great Pumpkin, rising up out of the pumpkin patch!" Linus yells. He is so excited to see the Great Pumpkin that he faints.

But it isn't the Great Pumpkin after all. It is just the World War One Flying Ace, on his way back from a very important mission.

Linus wakes up and asks Sally what happened.
"I was robbed!" howls Sally. "Halloween is over and I missed it!" She stomps out of the pumpkin patch, leaving Linus all alone to wait for the Great Pumpkin.
Linus falls asleep waiting, and later that night Lucy comes to bring him home and tuck him into his warm bed.

The next day, Charlie Brown tries to make Linus feel better. "Don't take it too hard that the Great Pumpkin never showed up," he tells his friend.

But Linus doesn't feel let down. "Just wait until next year!" he tells Charlie Brown. "I'll find the most sincere pumpkin patch, and I'll sit in that pumpkin patch until the Great Pumpkin appears!"